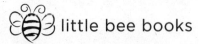 little bee books

An imprint of Bonnier Publishing USA
251 Park Avenue South, New York, NY 10010
Copyright © 2017 by Bonnier Publishing USA
All rights reserved, including the right of reproduction in whole or in part in any form.
LITTLE BEE BOOKS is a registered trademark of Bonnier Publishing USA, and associated colophon is a trademark of Bonnier Publishing USA.
Manufactured in the United States of America LB 0717

Library of Congress Cataloging-in-Publication Data:
Names: Pearl, Alexa, 1967– author.
Title: The Plant Pixies / by Alexa Pearl; illustrated by Paco Sordo.
Description: First edition. | New York: Little Bee Books, 2017.
Series: Tales of Sasha; #5 | Summary: Sasha learns what her special, royal power is when she tries to stop plant pixies from stealing feathers from the flying horses.
Identifiers: LCCN 2017004959
Subjects: | CYAC: Horses—Fiction. | Animals, Mythical—Fiction. | Princesses—Fiction. | Pixies—Fiction. | Friendship—Fiction. | BISAC: JUVENILE FICTION / Readers / Chapter Books. | JUVENILE FICTION / Animals / Horses. | JUVENILE FICTION / Animals / Mythical.
Classification: LCC PZ7.1.P425 Pl 2017 | DDC [Fic]—dc23
LC record available at https://lccn.loc.gov/2017004959

ISBN: 978-1-4998-0464-5 (hc)
First Edition 10 9 8 7 6 5 4 3 2 1
ISBN: 978-1-4998-0463-8 (pbk)
First Edition 10 9 8 7 6 5 4 3 2 1
littlebeebooks.com
bonnierpublishingusa.com

Tales of
SASHA

The Plant Pixies

by Alexa Pearl
illustrated by Paco Sordo

little bee books

Contents

Pixie in a Jar

"Let's talk pixie!" said Sasha.

Sasha wore a gold crown. It twinkled with white diamonds and pink crystals. Sasha was the Lost Princess of the flying horses.

Sasha hadn't always been a princess. She also hadn't always been able to fly.

Sasha grew up in Verdant Valley. She thought she was a regular horse, like all the other horses she knew.

Then one day, wings popped out. She could fly!

That was Surprise #1.

Sasha went to meet other flying horses that lived in Crystal Cove.

Then came Surprise #2. *She* was their Lost Princess. (Except now she wasn't lost anymore.)

Sasha had to pass a tricky test to get her crown. The flying horses said that passing the test would unlock her royal powers.

Now, Sasha was in a cave having a secret meeting with four other flying horses. They were the rulers of Crystal Cove. Sapphire was a kind blue horse. Xanthos was a serious yellow horse. Crimson was a proper red horse. Mercury was a quiet turquoise horse.

"What else can I do?" asked Sasha.

She could fly. Could she also read minds? Change into a dolphin?

"We don't know what else you can do," Sapphire told Sasha. "Your royal power is unique to you. It'll only appear when you need it most."

Sasha hated waiting—especially for good things like presents, birthdays, and royal powers. "I need it *now*. The plant pixies are on the move."

"Exactly!" Xanthos gave a loud whinny in reply.

Six hummingbirds flew into the cave. The hummingbirds were the flying horses' helpers. They held open a large map of Crystal Cove in their beaks.

"The plant pixies are dancing here," Xanthos said, pointing to a jungle on the map.

"The plant pixies are skipping here." He pointed to some mountains.

"The plant pixies are twirling here."

He pointed to a meadow.

"Soon, they will come *here*." He pointed to a beach.

Oh, no! Sasha gulped. The flying horses lived in the caves along the beach on the map.

"The plant pixies are coming to steal our wing feathers," said Crimson.

"We must stop them," said Sasha.

"It won't be easy." Xanthos brought her to a nearby shelf that held a large glass jar.

Sasha pressed her nose to the glass. A little fairy face stared back at her! A plant pixie!

The plant pixie had a pointy nose, pointy ears, and a pointy chin. Her skin was light purple, and her hair was long, flowing, and the color of grass. Her dress was made of tiny leaves.

"Her name is Collie." Xanthos pointed to a tiny necklace around her neck that spelled *Collie* in fancy script.

Collie sat cross-legged on a leaf at the bottom of the jar. A tiny tear trickled down her cheek.

"Oh, poor pixie," cried Sasha. "Why is Collie trapped in a jar? She looks so sweet."

Xanthos snorted. "Don't be fooled. Watch this."

He unlatched the lid from the jar. He slid a horse feather inside and touched Collie with its tip.

She startled and cried out.

Whoosh!

Thick vines sprouted from Collie's wrists. They grew and grew, twisting and climbing. They shot toward the top of the jar. Collie scampered up the vines like a rope. Her hazel eyes shone brightly. She was very near the top. Soon, she would be out of her glass prison.

The pixie was about to escape!

Bam!

Xanthos slammed down the lid.

The vines disappeared. Collie fell back onto the leaf. She rested her head in her tiny hands.

"That was mean," Sasha told Xanthos.

"Plant pixies are dangerous. I wanted to show you that," said Xanthos. "When they're scared or upset, they grow vines."

"What's so bad about vines?" asked Sasha.

"They use the vines to travel and to trap us," he explained.

Sasha peered through the glass. Collie was the size of a horsefly. Sasha was the size of a horse.

"She's too little to trap me."

"Pixies don't work alone. They travel in large groups," he said. "They surround a flying horse and tangle her up with thick vines. Then they pluck out two feathers."

Sapphire stepped closer to explain. "Plant pixies don't have wings of their own. See that harness they wear?"

Sasha spotted a tiny silver harness on Collie. It wrapped around her waist and strapped over her shoulders.

"If she puts two horse feathers into the harness, she can fly," said Sapphire.

"Is that so bad? It's only two feathers," Sasha pointed out.

"Only two? CLEMENTINE!" roared Xanthos.

A horse limped into the cave. Her orange coat was dull. Her eyes were cloudy. She wheezed and coughed.

"Oh, dear. What's wrong with her?" Sasha moved away.

"Clementine was healthy yesterday. Then the plant pixies used their vines to take two of her feathers. Today, she is weak and sick," said Xanthos. "Now the pixie can fly, but *she* can't."

Suddenly, Sasha understood how serious a pixie attack was. She didn't want to get sick. "What do we do?"

"Call Bill," Xanthos instructed the hummingbirds.

"Who's Bill?" Sasha looked around.

"I am Major Bill, your highness." A billy goat entered the cave. Military medals hung from ribbons around his neck. He saluted Sasha. "I lead the goat brigade."

How wonderfully strange Crystal Cove is, thought Sasha. Winged horses lived in caves. Beavers paddled a ferry boat. Flamingoes played jump rope, spider monkeys rode scooters—and a billy goat was in charge of the guards.

Sasha waved her tail in his direction. "Nice to meet you."

"Major Bill, it's time to send the goats to the meadow," Xanthos said, tapping an area on the map.

"The goats are ready and hungry, sir." Major Bill saluted again.

Why do we need a bunch of hungry goats? Sasha tried to puzzle it out.

She looked back at Collie inside the jar. The pixie wrapped the leaf around her tiny body, curling up inside it.

Then Sasha understood.

Pixies slept inside plants. Goats ate plants. The goats would destroy the pixies as they were resting. Sasha's stomach began to turn. "Wait! I don't want to hurt the little pixies."

"Plant pixies are enchanted. They live forever and ever. You can't really hurt them," said Xanthos.

"Then why send in hungry goats?"

"The goats' nibbling slows the vines from growing," said Xanthos. "The pixies use the vines to travel. This will keep the pixies from reaching our beach quickly."

"What do you say, Lost Princess?" asked Major Bill. "You wear the crown now. It's up to you."

Sasha watched Collie sleep. She remembered the climbing vines that shot from her wrists. She pictured hundreds of plant pixies, all with vines reaching for her wing feathers.

"I say . . . nibble away."

CHAPTER 3) Super-Flyers

"Come see!" Kimani poked her purple head into the cave. She was Sasha's best friend in Crystal Cove. "The Super-Flyers are putting on an air show."

"What's a Super-Flyer?" asked Sasha.

"I'll show you." Kimani's braided tail twirled with excitement.

Sasha followed Kimani onto the beach. The sand glittered with gems and jewels. Horses of all colors craned their necks upward.

Sasha stared up, too. The sunset glowed pink and orange in the empty sky. What was she looking for?

Whoosh!

Six magnificent white horses zoomed across the sky. Their shimmering wings stretched wide. They dove and dipped. They twirled and swirled. They flipped and soared.

Faster and faster and faster.

Sasha didn't dare blink. She didn't want to miss anything.

One horse flew up. Another horse flew down.

Then the sky grew dark.

Soon Sasha couldn't see the Super-Flyers. "Is it done?"

"Wait for it." Kimani grinned slyly, as if she knew a secret.

"For what—? Oh!" Sasha gasped.

Each horse lit up. One, two, three, four, five, six. Their bodies glowed in the night. The horses flew, swirling light overhead.

Sasha's heart danced along with them. She loved their speed. Nothing stood in their way up there.

Then she thought of Collie. Collie was trapped inside a glass jar. A lump formed in the back of Sasha's throat.

"I'll be right back," she whispered.

Kimani nodded, her eyes never leaving the sky.

Sasha quietly made her way into the empty cave. The glass jar still sat on the shelf. Collie slept, using the leaf as a sleeping bag. Tiny air holes were poked into the jar's lid.

Sasha heard voices from outside. The Super-Flyers must be ending their show. *Will Collie be okay?* wondered Sasha.

She knew she shouldn't care. Collie was a plant pixie, and plant pixies were the enemies of the flying horses.

But she did care.

Suddenly, she heard voices getting closer. Xanthos and Sapphire would soon return. Sasha grabbed the jar's handle with her teeth. She hurried out and slipped into Kimani's cave for a sleepover they'd planned.

Now what? Sasha's heart beat fast.

She didn't dare take off the lid. Xanthos had said Collie was dangerous.

"Sasha? Are you in here?" Kimani called.

What would Kimani think about hiding a plant pixie? Suddenly, Sasha wasn't sure why she'd grabbed the jar. Had she done a good thing or a bad thing?

Sasha tucked the jar under her straw mattress.

"I'm here," Sasha told Kimani. "I was tired." Sasha yawned and realized she really was tired.

Sasha decided to keep Collie a secret for now.

She closed her eyes and went to sleep.

CHAPTER 4) So Much to Talk About

Hiccup, hiccup.

Sasha kept sleeping.

Hiccup, hiccup.

What was that sound? She opened her eyes. She looked over at Kimani, who was fast asleep.

Hiccup, hiccup.

The sound came from *under* Sasha. How could that be?

The jar! Quickly, she snatched it from under the mattress and then carried it outside.

The beach was quiet, except for the waves lapping onto the shore. The jewels on the sand glimmered in the pale moonlight.

Sasha rested the jar on a large rock. She peered inside.

Hiccup, hiccup.

Collie looked upset. She had the hiccups.

"Holding my breath helps them go away," said Sasha.

Collie waved a hand by her pointy ear. She couldn't hear from inside the jar.

Sasha puffed out her cheeks with air. She motioned for Collie to do the same thing.

Collie took a deep breath. She held it.

Hiccup, hiccup.

That didn't work. Sasha had another idea.

She raised her front hooves. She made a mean face, and her nostrils flared wide. "Ahhh!"

Collie hid her eyes in fright.

"Did I scare them away?" asked Sasha.

Hiccup, hiccup.

"I guess not." Sasha watched Collie's little body shake with each hiccup.

Then Sasha remembered how her mother placed drops of sweet morning dew under her tongue to chase away hiccups.

Dew dotted some nearby sea grass, but the only way to give it to Collie was to open the jar.

I'll do it superfast, decided Sasha.

She unlatched the lid and quickly placed the drops under Collie's tiny tongue. They waited together.

No more hiccups!

Her mother's trick had worked.

"Thanks a bunch." Collie's words came out like a song.

"You're welcome." Sasha went to put the lid back on.

"Please, don't leave me in here," begged Collie. "I'm so lonely."

"I can't just let you out."

"Can we just talk for a little bit?" Collie's emerald eyes widened. "I'm so far from home and from my family."

"Me, too. I miss my two sisters and my better-than-best friend, Wyatt."

"I have a sister, too. She washes my hair with nectar."

"My sister Poppy braids flowers into my mane and tail."

"What kind of flowers?" asked Collie.

"Mostly daisies."

Collie pointed to her dress. "Daisies are my favorite."

Sasha and Collie had so much to talk about. They talked about their sisters and their parents. Collie's mother was in charge of all the plant pixies.

"That makes you pixie royalty, like me." Sasha touched her crown, resting nearby. "Why are you in a jar?"

"I got tangled in the mane of a flying horse."

"What a strange place to be. What were you doing in someone's mane?" asked Sasha.

"Making it beautiful. Plant pixies make the world more beautiful. We sprinkle pixie dust on plants so flowers bloom and vegetables grow. We turn brown fields green. My talent is braiding. I do French braids, fish tails, and diamond braids."

"What's a diamond braid?"

"I'll show you. Help me get out of here, okay?"

Sasha hesitated.

"I won't hurt you. I only want to braid your mane," said Collie. "I've never stolen a feather. The other pixies think it's funny, because my mom is in charge. They laugh at me."

Sasha had been laughed at in school by the horses that didn't fly. She and Collie were a lot alike.

She helped Collie out of the jar.

CHAPTER 5) Enchanted Somersaults

Collie scampered into her mane. She sang softly as she braided.

The sun began to rise. Birds chirped to welcome the day.

Suddenly, their chirps turned into frightened squawks.

What's happening? Sasha turned and gasped. Goats were somersaulting toward her!

Kimani raced out of her cave. "The pixies enchanted the goats! The goats can't stop somersaulting."

They rolled in from the meadow, one after the other.

"It looks like the goat plan didn't work," said Sasha.

Major Bill rolled up to them. "Go inside! We don't want them to find you."

Sasha felt Collie nuzzle into her mane to hide. Then Kimani pulled Sasha inside her cave. Sapphire and Xanthos soon trotted in.

"Kimani, your room is so messy." Sapphire looked around. Crumpled blankets lay in heaps. Straw fell out of mattresses. Carrot cake crumbs littered the floor. "You must clean it before we allow you to fly again."

"No flying?" Kimani sounded sad.
"No flying," said Sapphire. She could take away flying because she was one of the rulers of Crystal Cove.

"Who cares about a mess right now? It's a pixie attack!" cried Xanthos. "The pixies want Sasha's royal feathers most of all."

"Why *my* feathers?" asked Sasha.

"Your feathers are more powerful than ours," Xanthos answered her.

A hummingbird flew in. The goats needed help. They were quite dizzy.

"Stay here. We'll talk about this later," said Xanthos. He, Sapphire, and Kimani hurried outside.

Sasha watched them go. Then Collie climbed out of her mane.

"Wow! It was hot in there." Collie stood between Sasha's ears. Then she slid down Sasha's nose and sat by her nostrils.

Sasha crossed her eyes to see her. "I'm glad they didn't find you."

"You're a good friend to keep my secret."

Sasha grinned. She liked being Collie's friend.

"I never knew that your feathers were more powerful than theirs." Collie swung her tiny legs. "You know, if I got your feathers, the other pixies would stop laughing at me. I'd be a hero. It's so easy, too. I mean, I'm standing right on top of the Lost Princess!"

Sasha's heart began to thump. *What have I done?* she thought.

Would Collie take her feathers?

"You need to go back inside the jar," said Sasha.

"No, I'm not leaving!" said Collie.

"You have to. I don't want you to take my feathers," said Sasha.

"Oh, snapdragon!" Collie giggled. "I was only joking. I won't really do it."

Sasha didn't know if she could trust her new friend.

"You need to get off now!" Sasha shook her head.

Collie grabbed onto Sasha's forelock. She held tight.

Sasha shook harder and harder.

Collie got scared. Vines shot from her wrists. They circled Sasha's ears.

Oh, no! thought Sasha. *I have to do something—fast.*

Ah-choo!

Sasha let out a huge sneeze, spraying Collie with snot.

The vines shrunk away. Collie lost her grip. She slid down Sasha's nose as if it were a waterslide.

Collie landed with a *splat!* on the ground. Sneeze-snot dripped from her shimmering green hair. "Gross! That wasn't nice."

Sasha mopped up the sneeze with her tail. "I'm sorry, Collie."

"You'll never believe this!" Kimani hurried into the cave.

"Hide!" Sasha nudged Collie under a blanket.

"The pixie ran away," said Kimani. "Her empty jar was found on the beach. Do you think she used magic to escape?"

Sasha took a deep breath. It was time to tell Kimani about Collie.

Before Sasha could begin her story, the birds outside began to screech loudly.

"It's the bird alarm! Let's go see." Kimani pushed Sasha toward the cave entrance.

Sasha looked down at the blanket. Would Collie be here when she got back?

Xanthos and Sapphire waited over on the beach as Kimani and Sasha walked outside. Mercury and Crimson hurried toward them.

"The grass in the meadow turned brown," said Mercury.

"And the flowers died," said Crimson.

Nobody knew why this had happened.

"The flying horses will have nothing to eat," said Mercury. Like all horses, the flying horses ate grass and wildflowers.

"We must find new green fields," said Xanthos. The four horses flew away.

"The plant pixies stopped spreading their pixie dust," Sasha told Kimani. "That's why the grass turned brown and the flowers won't bloom. They use pixie dust to make things grow and make the world beautiful."

"How do you know?" asked Kimani.

"I learned about the pixie dust from Collie," Sasha answered.

"You *talked* to her?" Kimani's eyes bulged with surprise.

"Yes. Why are you looking at me like that?"

"No flying horse has ever spoken to a plant pixie before. We don't speak the same language as they do. Their language makes no sense to us."

"It makes sense to me," said Sasha.

"That's amazing." Kimani shook her head with wonder.

"You should meet Collie," offered Sasha.

"Meet her?" Kimani sounded scared. "Isn't she dangerous? Won't she hurt us?"

"Not at all. She's very nice," said Sasha. "I hope she's still here."

Sasha led Kimani back inside the cave.

"Oh! *Who* did this?" cried Kimani.

Her cave was now sparkling clean. The blankets were folded. The pillows were stacked. The straw had been stuffed back into the mattresses. Kimani's hair ribbons were braided into streamers. The air smelled like lilacs.

Did Collie do this? wondered Sasha. She knew Collie loved to braid.

"Collie?" Sasha looked for her. "Kimani wants to meet you. Are you here?"

CHAPTER 7) Keeping Up with the Pillywiggins

"Hi, it's nice to meet you." Collie stepped out from behind a big pillow and greeted Kimani.

"I didn't hear words, just squeaks," Kimani told Sasha. "What did she say?"

"She said hello." Sasha turned to Collie. "Did you clean up?"

"Plant pixies love to tidy up. I made the cave beautiful because you let me out of the jar." Collie smiled warmly. "I didn't want your friend to be sad."

Sasha smiled. Collie *was* a good friend. Kimani twirled her tail with excitement. "Sasha! I think we found your royal power."

"We did?" asked Sasha.

"You're the only one in Crystal Cove who speaks the pixie language. I bet you can understand elves and fairies, too. That's your power!"

Sasha had hoped for a more exciting power. "What good is talking to plant pixies?"

"You can ask them things."

"What kind of things?"

"You can ask them things like why they're stealing our feathers," said Kimani.

"It's because they want to fly," Sasha explained.

"But why?" asked Kimani. "We have no idea."

Sasha blinked. How strange! The plant pixies were the enemies of the flying horses, but they had never spoken to one another.

"Collie, why do the plant pixies want to fly?" asked Sasha.

"Flying is cool as a cucumber!" She clapped her hands in delight. "At least, I think it is. I've never done it."

"That's the whole reason?"

"No." Collie grew serious. "The pillywiggins are the reason."

Sasha was confused. "What's a pillywiggin?"

"Pillywiggins are smaller than pixies. They sleep inside tulips. They wear acorn caps and have butterfly wings. They fly from flower to flower and drink nectar out of tiny straws."

"That's so sweet," said Sasha.

"Not to a hungry pixie. We must climb the stems to reach the flowers. Have you ever tried that? It's really hard! By the time we get there, the pillywiggins have slurped up all the nectar," said Collie.

"Is that why the plant pixies take our feathers? So they can fly from flower to flower like the pillywiggins?" guessed Sasha.

"Yes, exactly!" said Collie.

"The flying horses and the plant pixies don't need to fight. We can find a way for the plant pixies to fly—just not with horse feathers," Sasha told Kimani. "Let's go on a wing hunt."

"I'm going, too. Coming up, buttercup!" Collie scampered up Sasha's leg. She hid inside her mane.

They both flew off in search of wings.

Wing Hunt

They flew above the beach. Sasha felt Collie's little hands braiding her mane.

Kimani pointed. "The peacock down there is standing by . . . a large pile of feathers!"

They flew down.

"Are those feathers yours?" asked Kimani.

"I'd say so." The peacock puffed out his chest. "Every year, I shed my old feathers and grow new ones."

"Can we take them?" asked Sasha.

The peacock nodded. "Sure! Out with the old and in with the new!"

After the peacock strutted away, Collie climbed out. She inserted two peacock feathers into her silver harness. She pulled a tiny cord, and the feathers began to flap.

Collie flew off the ground. It was working!

She hovered for a minute, but she couldn't fly higher than Sasha's knees.

"They don't have enough flying power," said Collie.

"A peacock's feathers are about beauty and not about flying," said Sasha.

At that moment, a toucan flew by. His shiny black feathers were perfect for flying.

Kimani waved him over to join them. She asked if they could pluck some of his feathers.

"No way!" said the toucan.

"That's okay," Sasha told Kimani. "We need feathers for *all* the plant pixies. He'd be bald if he gave us that many."

They searched up and down the beach. There were no feathers to give the plant pixies to be found.

Soon, it was lunchtime.
A platter waited in
front of Kimani's cave.
Usually, it was piled
high with wildflowers,
sweet grass, and fruit.
Today, it held only
gray mushrooms.

Kimani wrinkled her nose. "I guess
the plant pixies still haven't sprinkled
their pixie dust. This is all we have to
eat. Yuck."

Sasha took a bite. "These are drier than sand."

Kimani gave a whinny. Two hummingbirds appeared. They asked what they could do.

"A spritz of sweetness, please," she told them.

The hummingbirds drizzled nectar on the mushrooms with their long, skinny beaks.

Sasha took another bite. "So much tastier!"

"The hummingbirds are the best. They help the flying horses in every way," said Kimani.

"In . . . every . . . way?" Sasha repeated slowly. "I've got it!"

Sasha whispered her new idea into Kimani's ear. She'd had many ideas today, but her new idea was better than all of them!

Sasha and Kimani spoke to the hummingbirds. Then Sasha called Collie to come out.

Collie quickly licked the extra nectar off the platter. "Delicious!"

"We have to try this before anyone sees you," said Sasha. "Climb on top of a hummingbird."

"Poppin' poppies, that's crazy!" Collie crossed her little arms across her chest.

"The hummingbirds fly. You want to fly. They are small. You are small, too. It's the perfect pair."

"I don't like pears," said Collie.

"Not that kind of pear. A duo. A team," explained Sasha. "You can ride on her back."

Collie climbed on. She wrapped her silver harness around the hummingbird's neck, making a bridle and reins.

"Let's do this," Collie said, holding on tight. "Up, up, and away!"

The hummingbird beat her wings. She rose into the air—bringing Collie to the nearest flower. She hovered there, as Collie stepped off the tiny floating creature and onto the petals. Collie took a big drink of nectar. Then she scampered back onto the hummingbird.

"That was awesome!" cried Collie. Sasha and Kimani cheered.

"Here's the deal," said Sasha. "The hummingbirds will give the plant pixies rides to the flowers. They are faster than pillywiggins, so you'll get *a lot* of nectar. If they do this, the plant pixies must agree to never take another feather from a flying horse."

"I'll go tell my mother this plan and ask what she thinks," said Collie. "Root for me!"

CHAPTER 9) Make Like a Tree and Leave

Sasha and Kimani searched the sky. "Don't worry, she'll be back."

Sasha had been saying this all afternoon. Now the sun was starting to set, and Collie and the hummingbird still hadn't come back. Were they lost? Had Collie's mom hated her idea?

Xanthos and Sapphire galloped onto the beach toward them.

"You shouldn't be out here. It's not safe," said Sapphire.

"Tell them about the plant pixie," Kimani urged Sasha.

"*What* plant pixie?" asked Xanthos.

"The one in the jar." Sasha told them everything. She explained about her royal power to understand pixie language. She told them about pillywiggins and hummingbird rides. She told them about her new friend, Collie.

"It won't work." Sapphire shook her head. "Flying horses and plant pixies can't be friends."

"Oh yes, they can!" Collie swooped down out of the sky on the back of the hummingbird. She held the reins with one hand and waved to Sasha with the other.

"You're here!" Sasha was so happy to see her.

"My mother loves the hummingbird idea. You have a deal. We will leave your horse feathers alone forever." Collie grinned. "Guess what, Sasha? I'm a hero. All the pixies cheered for me!"

Sasha cheered for her, too.

"What's she saying?" asked Sapphire.

"The pixie problem is over. The flying horses are safe!" cried Sasha.

Now everyone cheered.

Mercury and Crimson galloped over as Major Bill joined them. "The fields are green again! The flowers are blooming!"

"The plant pixies did that," Collie told Sasha. "We stopped the goats from somersaulting, too."

Sasha raised a hoof. Collie slapped her a high-five.

Kimani called over all the hummingbirds. The plant pixies were now gathered together, waiting in the meadow. Each plant pixie would pick a hummingbird to be his or her partner.

"Can I be partners with you?" Collie asked the hummingbird she'd been riding.

"I'd like that," replied the hummingbird. "My name is Lucia."

Xanthos took one of the medals that hung around Major Bill's neck and put it around Sasha's neck. "Sasha's royal power and smart thinking saved the flying horses. We can now fly anywhere we want."

"I'm flying home to Verdant Valley," Sasha said, turning to Collie. "Do you want to meet my sisters?"

"Yes!" said Collie. "Let's make like a tree and leave."

"Can I come, too?" asked Kimani.

"I want all my friends with me." Sasha flapped her wings and soared through the clouds.

Kimani flew next to her.

Collie leaped onto Lucia, and they took to the air. The plant pixie flew alongside the two flying horses.

"Wait! Stop!" Sapphire zoomed up to them. "You need to go to the Royal Island of Flying Horses."

"Where is the island?" Sasha had never heard of it before.

"Under the clouds, around the rainbow, and over the sea," said Sapphire.

"But why? What's there?" asked Sasha.

"Someone special is waiting there for you," said Sapphire.

Read on for a sneak peek
from the sixth book in the
Tales of Sasha series!

Tales of SASHA

Wings for Wyatt

by Alexa Pearl

illustrated by Paco Sordo

Lucky Charm

"I'm not going," said Sasha. Her words echoed across the sky.

The yellow flying horse stopped talking. The purple flying horse stopped laughing. The green flying horse stopped singing. They all flew closer to Sasha.

Sapphire circled Sasha. Her blue coat gleamed in the sun, and she frowned. "What?"

Sasha flapped her wings quickly to hover in place. She was nervous. Sapphire ruled the flying horses. No one ever refused her orders.

Until now.

"I'm not going to the Royal Island," Sasha said, trying to make her voice sound strong, even though her knees wobbled. "I can't."

Sapphire's bright blue eyes narrowed.

"Why not?"

"I miss my family," Sasha said with a gulp. "It's been so long since I've seen them."

Sapphire's frown went away. Her voice softened. "We're your family, too. Your flying family."

"You're our Lost Princess," added Sasha's friend Kimani. She flew up beside her. "We need you."

Sasha's head was spinning. So much had happened so fast.

Only a little while ago, she was living in Verdant Valley with her parents and two sisters. She had known she was different than the other horses, but she couldn't figure out how. Then one day, wings popped out of her back. She could fly!

Sasha was a flying horse.

Soon she learned that other flying horses

lived in Crystal Cove. Sasha traveled to meet them. She discovered she was their Lost Princess! They had left her with a family of regular horses when she was a baby. They had wanted to keep their princess safe from the plant pixies.

Now the plant pixies and the flying horses were friends thanks to Sasha. She'd fixed everything with her special Lost Princess powers. Sapphire wanted Sasha to go to the Royal Island to meet someone important. She wouldn't tell Sasha who it was yet.

Sasha was curious, but . . . the island was far away out in the sea.

Sasha missed her family in Verdant Valley. She missed her friends. She missed the green fields and even her lessons at school.

Sasha wanted to help the flying horses. She also wanted to give her mom a big nuzzle.

"I don't know what to do," Sasha said to Sapphire. "I have two families now."

"The more family, the more love." Sapphire looked to the sky. "The best time to fly to the island is when a rainbow fills the sky. The sun will shine today and tomorrow. Then the rain and the rainbow will come. You can go to Verdant Valley before going to the island."

"Thank you!" cried Sasha. She promised Sapphire she'd go to the island as soon as the rainbow appeared.

"I can't believe she's letting you go." Kimani looked shocked. Sapphire never changed her mind.

"We're so lucky Sasha came back to us." Sapphire untied a long, thin, black velvet ribbon with a small gold star attached to it from around her tail.

"What is that?" asked Sasha.

"A lucky star," Sapphire said, tying it to Sasha's gray tail.

"Oh, I want a lucky star, too," cried Kimani.

"This star brings luck *only* when worn by a royal horse, like Sasha," said Sapphire.

"Why do I need luck?" asked Sasha.

"Flying around the rainbow to the island is tricky." Sapphire touched the star. "This lucky star will keep you safe. Make sure you travel with it."

Sasha had never had a lucky charm before. She swished her tail to show it to Kimani.

"It's so sparkly!" said Kimani. She smiled at Sasha.

"Are you ready?" asked Sapphire.

"I am!" Sasha said goodbye to all the flying horses. Then she opened her wings wide and soared across the sky. She was going home.